Goran's Great Escape

Astrid Lindgren • Marit Törnqvist

Floris Books

This is the story of Goran the bull, who escaped from his barn one Easter Day, many years ago. He might still be free, if only … Let's find out what happened.

Goran was a huge bull. He lived in a barn in Sweden, with rows of cows and their little calves. Goran was usually a good-natured bull. The farmhand who looked after the animals in the barn was also kind. He was called Svensson. He was so kind that one time when Goran accidentally stepped on his foot, Svensson didn't have the heart to push him away. He just stood there patiently until Goran decided to move.

But on this Easter Day, Goran was angry. You could ask why he was in such a terribly bad mood that day. We will never know. Perhaps one of the calves had said something rude to him, or perhaps the cows had teased him.

In any case, that Easter morning, Goran decided to escape. He thundered down the barn with such a terrible look in his eye that Svensson didn't dare to stop and ask him what was wrong. Instead, he ran for his life, out the barn door. Goran chased after him in a wild rage.

Outside the barn was a yard, surrounded by a fence. Svensson ran through the gate and slammed it shut on Goran's nose as the bull prepared to charge at his old friend.

It was, as you know, Easter Day, and the farmer and his family were eating their breakfast in the farmhouse in peace and quiet. It was a beautiful day and the farmer's children were happy, not because they were going to church for Easter, but because they all had new shoes to wear, and because the sun was shining, and because they were going to play in the stream by the meadow later that afternoon.

But that never happened. None of their plans happened, because of Goran.

Down in the farmyard, Goran was charging around, bellowing madly.
Svensson looked at him helplessly from the other side of the fence, trembling
with fright.

Soon everyone rushed down to the farmyard — the farmer and his wife,
the children, the servants and the farmhands — to watch the angry bull.
By then, the news had spread throughout the countryside: a prize bull was
running around like a roaring lion.

People came from all the houses and cottages for miles around, eager to watch the drama unfold. They were all glad of a little excitement to liven up a long, quiet Easter Day.

Karl was one of the first to come running, as fast as his small seven-year-old legs could carry him. He was a little Swedish farm boy, exactly like a thousand others — with blue eyes, blond hair and a runny nose.

By now, Goran had been loose for two hours, and no one had been able to calm him down. The farmer decided to try. He stepped through the gate and into the yard, and took several determined steps towards the bull.

This was a mistake. Goran had decided to be angry this Easter Day and he was going to stay that way. He lowered his head and charged, and if the farmer hadn't been such a good runner, who knows what might have happened. As it was, he tore a hole in the seat of his best Sunday trousers as he ran back through the gate. The spectators looked at one another and smiled quietly.

What a silly situation!

The cows began to moo in the barn. It was time for their midday milking. But who would dare cross the yard to get to them? No one.

"What if Goran stays angry forever, as long as we live?" said one little boy. That was a sad thought. They wouldn't be able to play hide-and-seek in the barn on winter evenings any more.

Easter Day stretched on. The sun shone, the sky was blue, the first leaves were appearing on the trees, everything was as delightful as it can be on an Easter Day in Sweden, but Goran was still angry.

There were anxious discussions on the other side of the fence. If someone could get near Goran with a long pole, perhaps they could hook it into his nose ring? Or maybe they would be forced to shoot him if he stayed so angry?

The cows mooed loudly. Something had to be done.

Karl, the little runny-nosed farm boy, was sitting on the fence.

"Goran," he said, "if you come over here, I'll scratch you between your horns."

If Goran understood him, he didn't pay any attention. Not to begin with, anyway. Because he wanted to be angry. But he heard that sweet little voice, over and over again, "Come over here, Goran, and I'll scratch you between your horns."

Perhaps, in the end, being angry wasn't as fun as Goran had thought it would be. He began to hesitate. And as he hesitated, he walked towards Karl.

Karl scratched Goran between the horns with his small, dirty, farm-boy fingers, while speaking friendly words.

Goran seemed a little embarrassed to be standing still, letting his head be scratched. But still he stood. Then Karl took a firm grip of Goran's nose ring and climbed over the fence into the yard.

"Have you lost your mind, boy?" someone shouted.

Slowly and carefully, Karl led Goran by his nose ring up to the barn door. Goran was a big, big bull, and Karl was a small, small boy. They made rather a touching pair as they walked across the yard. Those who saw it never forgot.

A Spanish bullfighter could not have received more claps and cheers than Karl did when he came out of the barn after leading Goran to his stall. Yes, claps and cheers, two coins and a dozen eggs in a bag were the young bullfighter's reward.

"I'm used to bulls," explained Karl. "You just have to be nice to them."

Then Karl turned round and went home, with two coins in his pocket and a
bag of eggs in his hand, quite satisfied with his Easter Day.

There he goes, a small Swedish bullfighter among the pale, pale green birch trees.